Volume 2, Number 2, published from time to time for the Hyborian Legion, other Conaniacs, and all admirers of the thunder-swashbuckle-fantasy type of adventure story.

ARTWORK

Stony Brook Barnes - - - - - 7
Irene L Brown - - - - - - - - 18
Juanita W Coulson - - 11, 12, 15
Robert E Gilbert - - - - - 4, 5
G H Scithers   1, 2, 7, 9, 10

CONTENTS

ART EDITOR
Dan Adkins

Second printing: 1974, $1.00.
Amra, Box 8243 Phila PA 19101

This thing is devised and propagated from and in the vicinity of Box 682, Stanford, California, to which address all money, manuscripts, comments, money, artwork, bombs, and money should be sent. Price - twenty ¢ per copy, one $ for a subscription of five issues. Foreign subscriptions, 25 ¢ and a $ for four (which exactly covers the extra postage and envelope required) British agent, John Dolittle, M.D., Puddleby-On-The-Marsh, Bristol.

BLUNDERS

This is supposed to be next issue – not this one, but things got a bit confused, and . . . Well, maybe we'd better start at the beginning and get this all down straight. As a matter of fact, things always seen a bit mixed up at this point, since this column, and the table of contents are the first things in the magazine, and are the last to be typed.

Anyway, we gathered together an issue – it was supposed to be this one, but more on that later. The issue was to consist – or rather will consist – of Poul Anderson's article, WHO WERE THE AESIR, Buck Coulson's short piece, CONAN: A SOCIAL COMMENTARY, the Miller-Clark-deCamp item, AN INFORMAL BIOGRAPHY OF CONAN THE CIMMERIAN. However, the INFORMAL BIOG was delayed (P Schuyler Miller is working on a re-write of it), the Anderson and the Coulson articles were sent out to be illustrated and haven't come back yet, and so on.

Meanwhile, back at Box 682, we had been accumulating material for the next issue. About a week ago, we suddenly realized that we had just enough for a complete issue – so here it is. It must be clearly understood, however, that this is really supposed to be next issue, and what was supposed to be this issue will come out in a month or so.

We would like to call your attention to the advertisements scattered throughout this issue. We will, with great pleasure, continue to take ads, charging fifteen cents per line, or a dollar per quarter page. (Anything from eight to thirteen lines costs a dollar, from four-lines to twenty six lines costs two dollars, and so on.) We are also most willing to accept almost any number of subscriptions – not so much because we are mercenary as because with our present number of subs, we are losing entirely too much money on each issue. Unlike some fanzines, our printing costs are such that the more subs we get, the less money we lose.

As for our costs – each issue cost us about twenty dollars to print and about seven dollars to fold, plus about a dollar for multilith mats. Each copy of an issue costs, in addition, about five cents for paper, and three for postage. (Printing costs and folding costs do not vary much with the size of the print order.) To add four pages (and we can add only in multiples of four) costs about four dollars for printing and one cent per issue. If we get more subs, we will probably do this – for the time being, it'll have to wait.

Some questions have been raised about who is editing this magazine. Actually, there is a board of us. consisting of indefinitely many members – for example: **Dan Adkins**, Art Editor; Thomas Stratton, Barsoomian Editor; Elizabeth Wilson, Horse Editor; Karen Anderson, Rejection Editor; Justin Kidd, Advertising Editor; G H Scithers, Cover Editor; Glenn Lord, Additional Editor; Poul Anderson, AEsirian Editor; Robert E Gilbert, Swashbuckling Editor; Irene Brown, Dragon Editor; and many more. As a matter of fact, some of us are doubted to exist.
##########

There is perhaps no one better qualified to discuss both swashbuckling adventure stories and the magazine markets for same than August Derleth. This Sauk City, Wisconsin writer began his career in Weird Tales before the literary debuts of either Robert E Howard or Fritz Leiber; in later years, as an editor, he was the first to publish their stories in book form. Although famed as a regional novelist, poet, essayist, anthologist, and critic, Derleth's affinity for the weird and fantastic remains unchanged through the years. His keen understanding of the current market situation is ably demonstrated in the following article.
R Bloch

THE WHEEL TURNS
by August Derleth

The apparent disappearance of the magazine market for the swash-buckle-magic-sex type of adventure tale, of which the most popular examples have been R E Howard's Conan tales and Fritz Leiber's Fafhrd & the Grey Mouser stories, is very probably only a temporary situation. The wheel invariably turns, and what is at the bottom today comes to the top in a decade or two -- or less -- again, unless, of course, the material is strictly dated and thus outdated by technological or social progress -- such as my Gus Elker stories of bucolic comedy, which, though widely published in Household, Atlantic, Yale Review, Scribner's, Extension, Progressive Farmer, Farm Journal, etc. today find berths only in occasional textbooks for secondary school use or in the Scholastic Magazines, not because they have lost merit as stories, but simply because technological progress has brought about social changes. The structure of the backgrounds and social patterns in the Gus Elker stories is no longer widely recognizable to magazine audiences, however valid it is to readers of books, where "dating" is not an important factor.

Now, manifestly, this does not apply to adventure stories of the Conan and Fafhrd & the Grey Mouser type. Markets for these stories are temporarily limited because editors of today, caught in a fast chang-ing market between rising production costs and the competition of paperback books are trying desperately to please and hold a sufficient body of readers to assure some kind of continued publication for their magazines. Further, many of the current editors are newer, younger men who almost automatically look upon the popular trends of the past as the wrong trends for today. From an editorial perspective, this is perhaps more often right than wrong. Yet the fact remains that the swashbuckle adventure story, the picaresque tale, and similar stories do not date easily, any more than do non-science-fiction types of fantasy, which is currently enjoying a resurgence of popularity reflected in increased sales at Arkham House -- almost ten times in 1958 what they were in 1955, for example.

In this rising sales pattern, Howard's Skull Face and Others generally surpasses numerically most of the other Arkham House books, excepting only recent titles: in part this may be due to the fact that this title will soon -- or relatively soon -- be out of print (about 400 copies remain out of 3,000), but that alone does not explain an upsurge in popularity at this time, because there has also been an increase in sales in Leiber's Night's Black Agents, though not on the same scale as Howard's book. Tastes -- both editorial and reader -- vary from year to year less noticeably than from decade to decade. Just now science-fiction is on a diminishing curve; it will rise again, though I doubt that it will again reach the boom proportions it reached a decade ago. At the same time that science-fiction is going down in popularity, macabre fiction is rising.

It would be a mistake, however, to conclude that the decline in popularity of any one type of story is due to the lack of editorial acumen; editors have to be responsible people; if they are not, their jobs are at stake and their magazines may suspend. In the case of science-fiction, the magazines have to fight the competition of paper- back books, which are a larger factor than one might think. In the case of the picaresque or swashbuckle adventure tale, the limitation of markets operates against them, and this limitation is also in a very large part brought about not by a fundamental change in public taste but by the rising costs of production, and the competition of the paperbacks which now literally flood the newsstands as once the pulp magazines did.

REG

There is another factor to be considered, particularily in relation to book publication, and that is one usually ignored by enthusiastic newcomers to the field. It is that even at best there is a limited audience for any one type of fiction -- whether horror, science-fiction, whimsy, swashbuckle adventure -- and, when it comes to cloth-bound books at higher prices, that audience dwindles appreciably from the larger audience which can be counted upon to buy a paperback or a magazine. When interest in science-fiction burgeoned over a decade ago, I cautioned my competitors who talked enthusiastically of average sales of 100,000 and 150,000 per title that a 10,000 copy sale for an average was to be considered remarkable, and that anything over that was to be looked on as a decided exception to the average. The same thing is true of non-science-fiction fantasy -- an occasional anthology of weirds may sell as many as 150,000 copies even in hardbound form, but the average printing of an Arkham House collection in this genre is 2,000, which will take an average of ten years to sell out. This could be raised, and the sales could be expedited if it were possible and less costly to reach the entire potential audience, but it is simply not possible to do so, and for a publisher the time soon comes when the cost of the advertising outlay necessary not only completely engulfs his potential profit but puts him definitely in the red.

These are matters which many of my competitors did not forsee, and in consequence Arkham House is still cautiously but very much alive today, and these competitors are no longer publishing.

For the time being, the swashbuckle or picaresque adventure tale may be in eclipse, but the rising interest in macabre and strange tales of all kinds will certainly bring renewed popularity to this kind of tale, which, after all, has its appeal primarily to every red blooded reader, and is not limited only to devotees of the supernatural. It would be a mistake to think of the eminently readable Fafhrd & the Grey Mouser or Conan tales only as exercises in magic; indeed, the fantastic elements in these stories have consistently been subordinated to imaginative adventures and to action in a far greater proportion than one generally finds in a macabre tale.

Patently, writers must write what sells -- but I always hope that writers with such veins as Leiber has developed in his Fafhrd & the Grey Mouser series will not abandon them. I write children's books which sell well, but I also write the Solar Pons pastiches, which have never sold particularily well but seem now to be catching on. There are all too few writers who can do sucessfully what Howard did in his Conan series or what Leiber has done and can continue to do in the Fafhrd & the Grey Mouser stories.

One must patiently upon the wheel to turn, for turn it will.

                                                              ##########

During his all too short career as editor of Unknown, John W Cambell, Jr. used in that much missed magazine not only the whackily humorous story that has become known as the Unknown type, but also he printed many stories of the swordplay-magic type. When we asked Mr Campbell to add something to the discussion of the market for this latter type of story he said he wouldn't do an article, but that he had a few comments on the subject. By the time he had finished writing his comments ...

John W Campbell, Jr.:

HEROES ARE OUT OF DATE

Mr Derleth has, I think, made a significant error of evaluation. He's quite correct in speaking of Gus Elkar bucolic-humor stories going out of date due to changing times and customs... but quite incorrect in saying that the swashbuckler hasn't gone out of date. The climate of the times has changed, and changed violently, in that regard.

The essence of it is this: last generation, there still remained a nostalgic feeling for the Hero -- for the man who was a Man, and more than ordinary run-of-the-mill people.

Today, the psychological and sociological climate is not merely uninterested -- it is very positively oriented against such characters.

A man who stands head-and-shoulders above ordinary man is undemocratic, authoritarian, is self-seeking, displays a power-drive or power-hunger, lacks a true sense of togetherness and teamship, considers himself superior to others, and in other words can be, and is, accused of a whole collection of highly negative attributes.

STONY BARNES

Now, furthermore, any man who writes about such characters and shows them in a favorable light is, obviously, undemocratic, authoritarian-minded, self-seeking, a believer in superiority, has a suppressed power-drive, and variously lays himself open to insult, attack, and scorn.

The editor who publishes such material also exposes his... quote the above string of derogatory adjectives... by showing he approves of the author's approval of his heroic characters.

Remember that that anti-social, undemocratic, psychologically disturbed authoritarian, Conan, not only wanted to be a king over other men, but even worse and more damnable, displayed more-than-democratically-normal powers and abilities, and did become a king. This shows that he was an evil man, one who should be scorned and rejected. And such stories should not be published where little children might be misguided to the anti-democratic idea that exceptional abilities merit exceptional reward. Various professional organizations exist to prevent this sort of deleterious thing. Thousands of people are ready to react loudly to such attacks on the proposition that "There are no such things as superior individuals, or heros."

As an arbitrary, authoritan, self-seeking, power-minded, anti-hyperdomocracy man myself, I disagree. And I am, as witness recent Astounding's -- particularly I call your attention to DESPOILERS OF THE GOLDEN EMPIRE -- trying deliberately to sabotage the American Way of Life. At least, if the current idolization of the weak-tea-and-milk-toast personality is the American Way of Life, I'm going to do my damnedest to poison it.

Swashbuckling is out of fashion -- and Psychology, Sociology, and the current philosophy of what-is-good is doing everything possible to deny it ever existed! That's the major reason such stories aren't being published or written.

##########

We've long wondered why such a lovely tale as
Poul Anderson's THE BARBARIAN got kicked out
of his wife's magazines only to appear in a
fullfledged, paying magazine. Here is the
story as explained by Karen Anderson...

WHY I REJECTED MY HUSBAND
by Karen Anderson

I have published fanzines for six years, not very regularly but
with a certain stubbornness. Anybody can publish a fanzine, and some
people keep it up for years or even decades. Whenever I'm tempted to
abandon fanzine publishing I consider some of the long-haul publishers
and decide that I'm not going to let them outdo me. I refuse to go
gafia.

For this reason I'm constantly in need of material to publish. I
write as much as I feel like doing, and then try to scrounge more from
any handy suckers. I belong to two amateur press associations, and
have just joined a round-robin publishing club, so that merely to keep
my membership I have to publish at least twenty single-spaced pages of
original material a year. I'd prefer to publish at least four times
that much, but I can't get as much as I want, and certainly don't
intend to write it all.

Fortunately, almost as soon as I began to publish fanzines I took
the precaution of marrying a professional writer. With proper stimuli
(such as beer) useful responses can be provoked in this writer, and an
evening's drinking frequently results in enough material for a story
or article. Most such articles or stories -- and it's usually a story
-- will, when written up, go out to market. Sometimes, though, he
writes something for me to publish in one or the other of my fanzines.

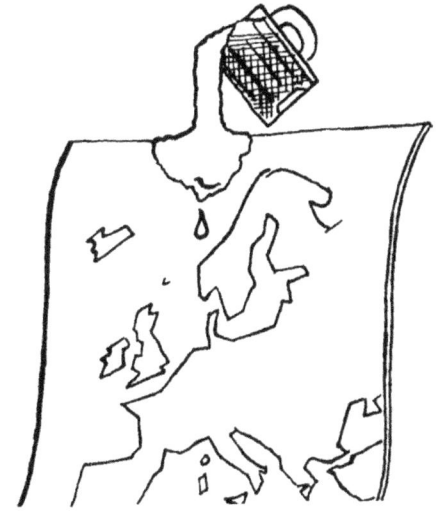

Naturally, I accept what he
writes for me almost without
question. It doesn't matter
whether it has anything to do
with science fiction. One of the
first things I published by him
was a beer drinkers' guide to
Europe, a careful and serious
collection of notes in which
he rated and described the
various beers he had encoun-
tered in England, France,
Germany, and Denmark. Another
was an ANGLO-SAXON CHRONICLE,
a simple description of nuc-
lear physics which used words

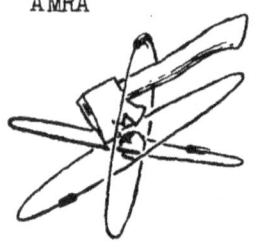

of Anglo-Saxon origin exclusively. (To give an idea of the effect, the title of the piece was UNCLEAVISH TRUETHINKING, meaning atomic theory.) Still another was a fanciful zoölogy dealing with fleishhackers, prompted by a visit to the Fleishhacker Zoo.

It's even better to have science-fictional material, though; I don't feel as a number of fanzine publishers do, that science fiction fandom is far more interesting and worthwhile than science fiction. I still consider fandom secondary to science fiction, and if I can get material about science fiction or fantasy, I'll print it in preference to material about fandom. And the best kind of all is a really good parody.

Well, he wrote me one once. He took the Conan stories and stood them on their head and tied them in knots. I read it and loved it all the way through. I enjoyed the basic premise and I enjoyed the specific details. It was just the sort of thing I wanted to publish, and I wish he'd write more like it.

Then I counted the pages.

Next I invited him to cut the stencils for me. He declined to do so.

I rejected the story. However, if you'd like to read it, you'll find it in the May, 1956, issue of The Magazine of Fantasy and Science Fiction.

I think the moral of the story is that everybody but me benefits from my laziness. But hang it all, I don't like to cut stencils!
— #########

ON THE TRUE CIRCUMSTANCES OF HOWARD'S DEATH

Somehow, beginning with the foreword to KING CONAN, the rumor has started that Howard drove thirty miles out into the desert and shot himself. Let me quote from the Cross Plains Review, 6/19/36...

Until Thursday of last week the young Cross Plains author had maintained an almost constant vigil at his mother's bed side. When her death became imminent he asked a nurse if she thought his mother would ever recognize him again.
Sympathetically, the nurse replied: "I'm afraid not."
Stoically, he rose from beside the sick-bed and walked to his automobile, which was parked to the side-rear of the Howard home. He got inside, closed the doors and fired a pistol bullet through his brain. Neighbors said the tragedy happened a few minutes after eight o'clock. He lived until four that afternoon.

And the country around Cross Plains is not desert. It is what might be called rolling hills covered with scrub oak and mesquite.

Glenn Lord, Box 775, Pasadena, Texas

JOHN CARPER AND HIS ELECTRIC BARSOOM

by

Thomas Stratton

(Reprinted from the July 1956 issue of <u>Yandro</u>)

Thomas Stratton is now 54 years old. He has had a wide
and varied career. His first job, at age 14, was that
of a grave-digger; since then he has been working his
way up through such varied tasks as house painter,
newspaperman, bookbinder, wool bagger, electrical
draftsman, and maintenance man for the Delco-Remy
plant in Kokomo, Ind. His fannish writing has appeared
in numerous Indiana fanzines, the most notable of
which are Merlin and Yandro; to the best of my knowledge this is the first time one of his stories has
appeared outside the state. He has hunted deer in Pennsylvania and gophers in the Silver Lake, Ind., ceme-
tery, ranked 25th in the 1957 state chess tournament,
is a member of a bowling team, absolutely nuts about
table tennis, and interested in stamp collecting, folk
music, and H. Allen Smith. At present, he lives noi-
sily (due to a fondness for full-volume hi-fi) in
Indiana with his wives and child.

*　　*　　*　　*　　*　　*　　*　　*　　*　　*　　*　　*

In a lovely golden garden in the capitol city of the country of
Hydrogen sat the bold heroic figure of John Carper, Jedackack of all
Barsoom, holding close to his bold heroic chest the pure and beau-
tiful form of his mate, the lovely Jedackackess of all Barsoom, Disha
Thorax.

They were, as one might expect of the Jedackack and Jedackackess
of all Barsoom, discussing the welfare of their loyal and devoted
subjects. They had been pursuing this patriotic line of discussion
for many hours when another bold heroic figure cleared the twenty-
foot garden wall in a leap and a half. It was, they saw as the figure
approached them in leaps and
bounds, revealing itself to
be not quite so bold and
heroic as John Carper himself, their only hatched son,
Cathartic.

"Father!" John Car-
per's son, the fruit of his
loins, cried, "I come to you
now to ask your aid, for you
are even more bold and heroic than I. That lovely
creature, second only in
beauty and purity to my
beloved mater, the fragile
and delicate Vethuvias, has
been taken captive, placed
in durance vile by the
infamous Tortoisians. She
-- oh vision of loveliness

JWC
2nd GREATEST WARRIOR ON ALL BARSOOM

that she is ! -- has been taken far across the dead sea bottoms to the
barren, wasted Polar Regions, the only place on all of Barsoom where
your power, oh bold heroic father, does not extend. So I ask of you
the boon of your incomparable succor in this hour of my greatest need
and sorrow."

John Carper, Jedackack of all Barsoom, disengaged himself gently
from the lovely arms of the beautiful Disha Thorax, and rose slowly
and thoughtfully to his feet. He looked at the noble countenance of
his only hatched son Cathartic, and seeing there the same Earthly
strain of courage, strength, and loyalty which flowed in his own noble
veins, made his decision. "Here, son," he said. "You may take my air
rifle and may all the gods of Barsoom go with you!"

"Oh great warrior and husband of mine!" spoke the incomparable
vision of beauty that was Disha Thorax, "do not jest at a time like
this! Do you not remember how you, John Carper, felt when I, Disha
Thorax, was torn from your bold heroic bosom when you first came to
Barsoom?"

"You are right, my beloved one," the Jedackack replied. He
turned again to Cathartic. "You may have the services of my army, and
my faithful friend and companion through all my intrepid adventures,
the six legged Barsoomian dog, Moola, will accompany you as will my
other loyal and beloved battle companion, that great green warrior,
Kars Karkas. This will, of course, leave the capitol city of Hydrogen
unguarded, but..."

The magnificent Jedackack of all Barsoom hesitated; modesty for-
bade him to continue. He motioned discreetly to the shimmering vision
of loveliness that rose gracefully from the ersatz bench. "But of
course," Disha Thorax continued, "Cathartic, my beloved and only-
hatched son, your father, being as bold and heroic as he is, will be
well able to hold off any trouble until you return with the army.
Besides, we killed off all our enemies in the last book."

"Electric Barsoom"--"Mars in a shocking state, perhaps?" Jean Bogert

Thus it was that, backed by the mightiest (in fact the only) army
on Barsoom and its third greatest warrior in the person of the giant
Kars Karkas, and led on by the keen sixth sense of smell of the
greatest Culotte of all Barsoom, Moola, Cathartic, the second greatest
warrior of all Barsoom, set out on his quest for the second loveliest
woman of all Barsoom.

Needless to say, he succeeded thumpingly.

Back across the red-crusted desert, the winding canals, the death-
less dead sea bottoms, wound the great retinue, carrying aloft on a
litter of gold and silver and precious stones, the fantastically
beautiful Vethuvias, lovely maid of Mars. Back to the capitol of
Hydrogen, where the great retinue lowered the litter of gold and
silver and precious stones with a sigh of relief and collapsed.

"Hail, Father!" spoke Cathartic. "I have succeeded in my quest for the second most lovely woman of Barsoom, and I return, grown greater in stature because of my recent valiant deeds."

"My only hatched son, it does my noble heart good to find that you are following in my bold and heroic footsteps. By the way, has your arduous journey diminished your princely strength in any wise?"

"No, father. I still feel that I am the second strongest mortal in Barsoom."

"Good. I have received disquieting reports concerning the legendary Puce Pirates of Phobos. How about running out there and checking up for me?"

"I am yours to command. Despite the fact that I have but returned from a cruel journey, and have only been re-united with the second loveliest woman in all Barsoom, I am ready to follow you to the end of the Universe!" ("And push you off," he added to himself.)

"Follow... Hmm.... well, that wasn't exactly.... oh, well, never mind. My son, with you beside me, nothing in the Universe can deter me."

Thus, as the golden orb of the sun rises over Hydrogen the next morning, we find a cavaran of Barsoomian flyers, bearing John Carper, Cathartic, Kars Karkas, Disha Thorax, Vethuvias, Moola, and scores of extras, also rising over the quiet city. John Carper, Jedackack of all Barsoom, has begun his quest for the Phantom Puce Pirates of Phobos, surely one of the strangest episodes in his gallant career!

The flyers rose higher in the Barsoomian morning; Disha Thorax and Vethuvias were sunning themselves on the top deck of the flagship, just in front of the flagpole. The glories of Barsoom spread out beneath the ascending ships. The magnificent, awe-inspiring dead sea bottoms were. What more need be said? Anyone who has had the inestimable privilege of viewing their grandeur has had the glorious magnificence of those incredibly awe-inspiring sights driven ineradicably into his mind, and no further word by me could in any way enhance those memories; and for those who have not, mere words could not do sufficient justice to those glorious monuments to the wondrous past of this ancient, time-honored planet.

Higher and higher still the flyers soared. The dead sea bottoms fell farther behind. Now the curve of the horizon could be seen, and the white glitter of the snowfields around the pole; the growing chill of the atmosphere forced Disha Thorax and Vethuvias to retire inside the flyer. Armed guards, shivering in uniforms more suited to the desert than this artic altitude (Barsoom had a lousy quartermaster service), patrolled the decks. Now, ahead of the valiant company, could be seen the jagged, snow-capped peaks of Phobos, the larger moon of Barsoom.

"Hold!" shouted John Carper, striding across the deck of the flagship. "Cease! Halt! Desist!"

VETHUVIAS
MADE
OF
MARS

The crew looked up from their various duties of patrolling the deck, steering, navigating, scraping barnacles from the hull and each other. "Sir," asked the captain, "what great wisdom and knowledge causes Your Imperial Jedackackishness to call upon this indomitable, invincible, indestructable, and altogether incomparable warfleet to stop?"

The Jedackack, suffering from one of his brilliant flashes of genius, replied, "Is this not a flyer? A flyer which requires air in which to fly? Is there air between Barsoom and Phobos? No! Therefore....."

"Father!" It was his only hatched son, Cathartic, standing before him on the wind-whipped airless deck. "You must have faith!"

The mighty John Carper appeared sad for a moment, then regained his Jedackackish composure. "You are right, my son! Sail on -- to the jagged snow-capped peaks of Phobos!"

But were these the jagged snow-capped peaks of Phobos? It has been truly said that faith can move mountains; but could faith put snow caps on mountains? Especially when there were no mountains there in the first place?

But of course! In a blinding flash of brilliant insight, it was all clear to John Carper: this was not Phobos before them! It was a cleverly constructed and camouflaged artificial moon, and the jagged snow-capped mountains were not jagged snow-capped mountains at all; they were in reality, he realized, ingeniously disguised gigantic weapons, the peaks being the deadly muzzles. And the Puce Pirates had those weapons trained upon them AT THAT VERY MOMENT!

All this he realized in less time than it takes me to tell it. [Anything takes less time than it takes you to tell it.] Even so, it was too late, for the brilliant flash, he also realized an instant later, was not from his scintillating intellect, but from the firing of those incredible weapons.

It was indeed fortunate for that gallant expedition that Cathartic had seen the danger a moment before. The flagship heeled sharply, and the bolts of ravening energy flashed past, scorching the paint on the bridge. At the same moment, Cathartic loosed a broadside from the port guns. Luckily, John Carper's hawklike eyes found it almost immediately. The entire fleet was now taking evasive action.

Flashing streaks of cosmic energy flamed between the fleet and the floating fort. With John Carper bellowing orders from the bridge of the flagship, the Barsoomian fleet began to close with the enemy. At last, two of the ships grounded on the artificial moon, and the Jedackack gave the order; "Boarders away!"

Swarms of chartreuse men, the deadliest fighters (except for John Carper and Cathartic) on Barsoom, poured onto the surface of the moon. Led by the bold and heroic Jedackack and his only hatched son, they were met by the Puce Pirates, and their allies, the magenta-and-heliotrope men of Deimos, in hand-to-hand combat. It was a colorful spectacle.

Meanwhile, back at the flagship, Vethuvias and Disha Thorax had crept quietly up the catwalk for a clearer conception of the cataclysmic chaos into which they had been catapulted. But no sooner had they at ained the deck of the craft than it tilted sharply sideways, dumping them precipitately onto the surface of the hostile artificial moon. The leader of the Puce Pirates, Argh Grghrd, took quick advantage of this by snatching them from under the very eyeballs of John Carper and Cathartic, not to mention Kars Karkas and the army, and swiftly secured them in his private quarters, inside the moon.

The battle raged on!

And on!

Finally, however, the smoke of battle (a spark from the clashing swords had started a fire) cleared away, and it could be seen that the forces of Evil had been crushed once more or less. Seeing their army destroyed, Argh Grghrd and his lieutenant, Mrumph, retreated below the surface of the moon.

Hot on the heels of the hellions hove the Heroes, hardly hesitating a hectare. (Barsoomian time unit barely worth mentioning.) Down through the labyrinthine, tortuous, twisting tunnels and carven passageways they battled; into depths lighted only by sparks from the clashing swords. At last, they arrived at the inner chambers where waited the two visions of beauty for which, subconsciously so far, this war (and countless others) had been waged and won.

As the two Heroes leaped into the room, Carper cried, "Unhand those visions of loveliness, you foul fiends, or you will have me -- and my only hatched son, Cathartic -- to deal with!"

"For that matter," added Cathartic, a practical soul, "you have us to deal with already."

"My bold heroic, only hatched son is correct," Carper affirmed. "And..." he gestured subtly to Disha Thorax and Vethuvias.

"And they are," chorused the visions of loveliness, "the mightiest fighting men on all Barsoom."

"True," admitted Argh, evincing more courage than was usual for those of his ilk, possibly because he had a small blaster trained on the mightiest fighting men of all Barsoom. "But," he continued, "you are not now on Barsoom!"

In a few moments, Barsoom had a new Jedackack.

#########

This (a preliminary report on a more complete discussion which will follow in the next issue) is a list of the Hyborian Kingdoms together with the modern political divisions to which they seem most closely to correspond, and is presented here as an aid to people wishing to pick the appropriate kingdom for their certificate of membership in the Hyborian Legion -- discussed at some length last issue.

THE KINGDOMS OF HYBORIA

Stephen F. Schultheis

AQUILONIA: New York
ARGOS: Virginia, N. Carolina, S. Carolina, Georgia
ASGARD: Norway, Sweden, Denmark
BARACHA ISLES: England
BORDER KINGDOM: Maine, Vermont, New Hampshire
BOSTONIAN MARCHES: Massachusetts, Connecticut, Rhode Island
BRYTHUNIA: Ohio
CIMMERIA: Canada
CORINTHIA: Kentucky
HYPERBORIA: N. Dakota, S. Dakota, Minnesota, Wisconsin, Michigan
HYRKANIA: Washington, Oregon, Nevada, Arizona
KHAURAN: Nebraska, Iowa, Kansas, Missouri
KHITAI: Northern California (see below)
KHORAJA: Oklahoma, Arkansas
KOTH: Tennessee
NEMEDIA: Pennsylvania
OPHIR: W. Virginia
PICTISH WILDERNESS: Ireland
POITAN: New Jersey
SHEM: Texas, Louisiana, Mississippi, Alabama, Florida
STYGIA: Mexico
TURAN: Montana, Idaho, Wyoming, Utah, Colorado, New Mexico
VANAHEIM: Parts of Europe not otherwise covered
VENDHYA: Southern California (see below)
ZAMORA: Illinois, Indiana
ZINGARA: Maryland, Delaware, District of Columbia

Vendhya covers the counties of Monterey, San Benito, Merced, Mariposa, Madera, Fresno, Inyo, and those south to the Mexican border. The rest of California is Khitai.

#########

CONAN & HIS WOMEN

by W H Griffey & Franklin Bergquist

For two people who have never heard of each other, these two come up with a pretty good, if inadvertent, collaboration...

Conan was no gentleman! Although we might surmise as much from his delight in hasty swordplay and his over-fondness for the wine when it was red, as well as his rough and ready use of fists to settle disputes -- there remains one main test by which we can be certain.

Gentlemen prefer blondes.

There are, in all, twenty-four published stories of Conan. Careful conning of them will reveal that the great warrior achieved feminine conquests in sixteen of these, there remaining eight in which no woman engrosses him.

In these conquests, which of the three main divisions of feminine loveliness -- blonde, brunette, auburn -- rated highest with our Hyborean champion? It would appear that black haired women were Conan's weakness. Out of the sixteen can be counted eleven brunettes and two redheads, while only three blondes made the grade. Considering that the famed Cimmerian came from a country of fair people with blue eyes, probably blonde although he was black haired himself, it is surprising to note that he went overboard so completely for dark haired women. Men usually become more interested in their opposites in the opposite sex.

Conan's disposal of his women is also rather mysterious. At the beginning of a story, he has sword, loincloth, perhaps some valuables borrowed without the owner's consent. At the end, he has sword, loincloth, valuables, and a girl on his arm -- a different girl for each story. Where do the women go between stories?

Perhaps Conan sold these women -- some of high degree -- as wives or slaves. Doing so would have furnished him with enough money to get to the place of his next adventure.

He could have done worse than selling them. Maybe he married them -- this would account for his being so frequently without funds. In fact, if he was henpecked, perhaps he traveled to get away from his wives. Possibly he was scared to death of women and simply put up a bold front until he could escape.

The answer to the mystery will be unknown unless some forgotten writings of Howard's are found, or unless someone else discovers the secret and, we hope, reveals it in some further adventures of Conan.

                                                    ##########

ARKHAM HOUSE: PUBLISHERS
Sauk City, Wisconsin

SKULL FACE & OTHERS, by Robert E Howard, $5.00
ALWAYS COMES EVENING, by Robert E Howard, $3.00
THE SURVIVOR AND OTHERS, by Lovecraft & Derleth, $3.00
THE FEASTING DEAD, by John Metcalfe, $2.50
THE CURSE OF YIG, by Zealia Bishop, $3.00
TALES FROM UNDERWOOD, by David H Keller, $3.00
NIGHT'S YAWNING PEAL, ed. by August Derleth, $3.00
THE HOUNDS OF TINDALOS, by Frank Belknap Long, $3.00
WITCH HOUSE, by Evangeline Walton, $2.50
THE HOUSE ON THE BORDERLAND AND OTHER NOVELS, by William Hope
        Hodgson, $5.00
THE DOLL AND ONE OTHER, by Algernon Blackwood, $1.50
WEST INDIA LIGHTS, by Henry S Whitehead, $3.00
FEARFUL PLEASURES, by A E Coppart, $3.00
THE CLOCK STRIKES TWELVE, by H Russell Wakefield, $3.00
THE NIGHT SIDE, ed. by August Derleth, $3.00
THIS MORTAL COIL, by Cynthia Asquith, $3.00
DARK OF THE MOON: Poems of Fantasy & the Macabre, ed. by August
        Derleth, $3.00
REVELATIONS IN BLACK, by Carl Jacobi, $3.00
THE WEB OF EASTER ISLAND, by Donald Wandrei, $3.00
"IN RE: SHERLOCK HOLMES" - THE ADVENTURES OF SOLAR PONS, by
        August Derleth, $3.00
THE FOURTH BOOK OF JORKENS, by Lord Dunsany, $3.00
GENIUS LOCI AND OTHER TALES, by Clark Ashton Smith, $3.00
ROADS, by Seabury Quinn, $2.00
NOT LONG FOR THIS WORLD, by August Derleth, $3.00
NIGHT'S BLACK AGENTS, by Fritz Leiber, Jr, $3.00
THE TRAVELING GRAVE AND OTHER STORIES, by L P Hartley, $3.00
THE MEMOIRS OF SOLAR PONS, by August Derleth, $3.00
SOMETHING ABOUT CATS AND OTHER PIECES, by H P
        Lovecraft, $3.00
THE THRONE OF SATURN, by S Fowler Wright, $3.00
THE DARK CHATEAU, by Clark Ashton Smith, $2.50
CARNACKI, THE GHOST-FINDER, by William Hope
        Hodgson, $3.00
SPELLS AND PHILTRES, by Clark Ashton Smith, $3.00
THE MASK OF CTHULHU, by August Derleth, $3.50
NINE HORRORS, by Joseph Payne Brennan, $3.00
THE RETURN OF SOLAR PONS, by August Derleth, $4.00
        --- Forthcoming ---
THE SHUTTERED ROOM & OTHER PIECES, by H P
        Lovecraft & Divers Hands, $5.00
THE ABOMINATIONS OF YONDO, by Clark Ashton
        Smith, $4.00

AMRA
BOX 682
STANFORD
CALIFORNIA
RETURN POSTAGE GURANTEED

MYCROFT & MORAN: PUBLISHERS
Sauk City, Wisconsin

www.ingramcontent.com/pod-product-compliance
Lightning Source LLC
Chambersburg PA
CBHW080906120626
46555CB00008B/2975